The Snow

Story by Rebecca Siddiqui

Illustrations by Samantha Asri

"Grandpa! Look at our bus,"
said Josh.
"It's going to be
a good snow bus!"

"No, it's not!" said Lily.
"It will not go down the path.
You are too heavy!"

"The bus will slide down a hill," said Josh.

"Grandpa," said Lily.

"Can we go up that hill?"

"Yes," said Grandpa.

"It's not too big."

"The hill looks bigger
from up here!" said Josh.
"It's a long way down."

"Who will go in the bus first?"
said Grandpa.

"I will," said Lily.
"I'm not heavy."

"Look out!" Lily shouted.

"Here I go!"

Lily went down the hill
in the snow bus.
She went faster and faster.

"Help!" laughed Lily.

"Josh! Grandpa!

I'm stuck in this hole

in the snow.

I can't get out!"

"We are coming!" Josh shouted.

Josh and Grandpa
ran down the hill.

They got the bus
out of the hole.

"Here I go again!" shouted Lily.
"I'm going very fast now!
This is lots of fun."

Lily went all the way
down the hill.

"Grandpa!" shouted Josh.

"Look at Lily.

She is in a snow plane!"